RUBY RED

TALES FROM THE

Henrietta Branford

Ruby Red

Tales from the Weedwater

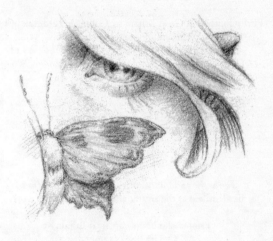

Illustrated by John Lupton

Collins

An imprint of HarperCollinsPublishers

First published in Great Britain by Collins in hardback in 1998
This edition published in 1999
Collins is an imprint of HarperCollins*Publishers* Ltd
77-85 Fulham Palace Road, Hammersmith, London, W6 8JB

3 5 7 9 8 6 4 2

Text copyright Henrietta Branford © 1998
Illustrations copyright John Lupton © 1998

ISBN 0 00 6752551

The author and illustrator assert the moral right to
be identified as the author and illustrator of the work.

Printed and bound in Great Britain by
Omnia Books Limited,
Glasgow G64

CONTENTS

FLOYD

RUBY

FERNANDA

FIRECRACKER

GARGOYLE

COLUMBINE · CRINKLE · CLUCK

FANCY
FOXY

GRANDMA
SAMPHIRE

SWEET
WILLIAM

BELLBINE

ROCKET

ROOKS

RUBY'S FRIENDS

RUBY'S FRIENDS

Ruby sat in the apple tree waiting for night to fall. It was midsummer's evening and the garden was quiet. Only the little River Weedwater still sang softly.

Three black rooks swung home across the sky. The Gargoyle watched them from his place above the door. He wished that *he* could fly.

The Gargoyle was Ruby's oldest friend. He had been down under the bright flow of the Weedwater for a hundred years when Ruby found him. She shook the caddis flies out of his ears, washed off the milfoil and carried him home. She fetched her ladder and her toolbox and fixed him to the wall next to a clock she'd found the week before.

Just at first, he felt kind of pointless up there.

"You should do something," Ruby told him. "Something important."

So she made him a wooden arm, hinged at the elbow, and a hand that could grip. She found him a mallet and a bell and she made a wind-up arrangement between his elbow and the clock's insides. After that the Gargoyle struck the hour, on the hour, every hour. And he never felt pointless again.

I go like clockwork, he thought, proudly. *Well, I am clockwork.*

Six was his favourite number. One and two seemed hardly worth bothering with. Nine and ten made his hinge ache. Six was just right. He smiled at Ruby in the apple tree and struck six.

"Thank you, Gargoyle," said Ruby, "I do like six o'clock – and now I always know exactly when it is." She climbed down and went indoors to cook her supper.

Ruby's hens flew up onto the garden gate and stared across the meadow to

Rook Wood. Dusk unsettled them. It made them dream of faraway places, of mystery and romance.

"Better shut ourselves up," Cluck sighed. "It's getting dark."

Crinkle and Columbine hurried into the coop. Cluck followed and fastened up the door. "Hungry old fox can sniff and snuff outside that door but he will not get in," said Cluck.

"Not a paw, not a claw," said Columbine.

"Never," said Crinkle.

Ruby leant out of the kitchen window. "Good night hens," she called. "See you in the morning."

She blew a kiss to the Gargoyle. "Good night," she called. "Sleep tight. Mind the fleas don't bite."

The Gargoyle frowned. He had not got fleas.

Ruby fetched wood and lit her fire. Smoke from the chimney made the Gargoyle sneeze. Ruby cooked buttered hop tops in a frying pan over the fire and ate them with a watercress salad.

After supper she took out her toolbox and worked on her latest invention. It was going to be a musical toaster.

Outside, beyond the firelight, woods and fields grew dark. Mice woke and went about their business – which was mostly food. Theirs, if they were lucky. Owl's, if he spotted them down among the grass stalks.

Presently, Ruby put away her toolbox and her toaster. She climbed the ladder to her bedroom, gave her hair a hundred brushes with a teazle head and lay down in her hammock. She read a page or two of her book by candlelight. Then she blew out her candle and slept.

Safe in their coop, Crinkle, Cluck and Columbine slept too.

High on the wall beside the clock the Gargoyle dreamed of church bells.

Deep down dark in the middle of the night, two yellow beams shone on the Gargoyle's face. He woke in a fright and struck twelve.

A van pulled up beside the meadow gate. *Titus Troy's Amazing Toys* it said on the side. An old man got out, went round to the back, and opened the doors.

Peeping out from a pile of broken toys was a little tin horse.

"King of the Toy Shop, you once was," said the old man, sadly. "Star Attraction. Always in the window."

The tin horse looked proud but said nothing.

"Toy Shop's shut now," the old man told him. "Business gone bust. Boss said to sell you lot for scrap."

The tin horse could not believe what he was hearing.

"But you deserve better than that. You want green grass under your hooves and blue sky above. That's why I brung you here."

The tin horse couldn't see where *here* was.

"So you can feel the wind blow.

Watch the sun go down of an evening and the golden moon rise up."

The old man lifted Floyd out and set him down in a corner of the meadow. Then he got back into the van and drove away.

The Gargoyle shut his eyes and slept.

Only the little moon, sleek as a minnow and curved at both ends, looked down on the tin horse standing so still in the meadow.

First up next morning was the sun who woke the birds and made them sing.

Second was the Gargoyle who struck six.

Third were the hens in their coop.

Fourth was Ruby who came out into the garden and sat down by the stream.

She dipped her bare brown feet in the water.

"Well feet," she said. "I wonder what today will bring?"

The tin horse could not see who was talking. He craned his neck but the hedge was too high for him. He tried to pick up his feet and trot to the gate but his knees were too stiff.

"I'm stuck," he said. "My knees won't bend."

Ruby ran to the gate and looked over. "Was that you talking?" she asked.

The tin horse looked all round the empty meadow. "No," he said. "It was me."

"Why don't your knees bend?" Ruby asked. "Mine do."

She did a few 'knees bends'. She

danced a little dance on the top bar of the gate – arms out, chin up. The tin horse watched admiringly. So did the Gargoyle. Crinkle, Cluck and Columbine tried a little dance of their own under the hedge.

"Now you try," Ruby said.

"I can't," said the tin horse. "I told you – I'm stuck."

Ruby fetched her oil can and rubbed oil into the tin horse's knees. She noticed a medal hanging round his neck. She rubbed that too. "F-l-o-y-d," she read. "Is that your name?"

The tin horse nodded. "Floyd the Mechanical Wonder Horse. That's me," he said.

Floyd, the Mechanical Rust Bucket, more like, the Gargoyle thought. Ruby had not so much as said 'Good Morning' to him.

Ruby tapped Floyd's joints with a little hammer. "I could make you as good as new," she said.

"Would it hurt?" he asked.

"Not as much as being all worn out."

"Being all worn out doesn't hurt. It's just a bit quiet."

Ruby fetched her toolbox and her work bench.

Floyd shut his eyes.

Ruby tightened his screws, adjusted his cogs and levers and polished him up to a dazzle.

"What you need now," she said, "Is a drop of my grandma's Elixir."

Ruby's Grandma Samphire had given her the Elixir. *One drop of this Elixir will*

Restore, Revive, Revitalise and Rejuvenate was written on the label. Ruby kept it in a special compartment of her toolbox, ready for emergencies. She took it out and shook it.

"What does it taste like?" Floyd asked.

"I've never tried it. You tell me." Carefully – because it isn't easy giving medicine to a horse – Ruby dripped a drop onto his tongue.

Floyd swivelled his ears. He swished his tail. He opened his eyes and shook his head and arched his neck. He neighed, rusty at first, then loud and proud. Away he went, high-stepping round the morning meadow while the webs of half-a-million spiders shimmered under his hooves.

Ruby ran after him. She climbed onto his back and stood, wobbling a little, on his smooth tin rump. She stretched out her arms to help her balance. The hens, perching on the top rung of the gate, held their breath as Floyd stepped out.

"That Ruby Red!" said Cluck.

"She's as bold as any hen!" said Crinkle.

"And just as elegant," said Columbine. "Look at her, Gargoyle!"

But the Gargoyle had screwed his eyes tight shut. He wouldn't look.

He couldn't bear to look in case his Ruby fell.

She didn't fall.

She never does.

Not Ruby.

SWAP SHOP

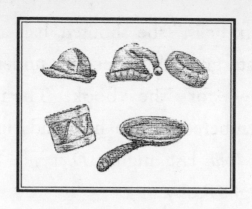

SWAP SHOP

Early one morning, just as the sun was rising, the Gargoyle struck six. Ruby sat up with a jump.

All night she'd dreamed of pirates on the Weedwater. She'd been reading a book called *Pirate Adventures of Fearless Fandango Fly* when she fell asleep. There was a picture of Fandango Fly on the cover. He had a parrot and a pigtail and he looked quite fierce.

"Six bells!" she shouted, half awake. "Pirate attack!" She felt under her pillow for the book. Then she remembered — she had read right to *The End* last night. *Drat my sprats!* thought Ruby.

She ate a clover pancake for breakfast and went to find Floyd. He had built himself six jumps and was trying for a clear round. "Watch me, Ruby!" he called. "See me go!"

I wish you would, thought the Gargoyle. Ruby had forgotten to say 'Good Morning' again.

Ruby waited till Floyd was between jumps. "Have you got any good books Floyd?" she asked. "Because I've read all mine."

Floyd hadn't. He didn't much like

reading.

The Gargoyle knew all about books and where to get them. But he said nothing.

Ruby thought there might be some books in her attic. It was full of boxes and Ruby opened the first one she came to. This is what she found inside:

three velvet hats
a drum
a frying pan
a wasps' nest
three bats, all sleeping
two boots and one shoe
six packets of seeds
a pair of red brocade ice skates

But no books.

Ruby dug in her garden all morning while Floyd jumped clear rounds in the meadow and the Gargoyle stared at the horizon.

When the Gargoyle struck twelve, Ruby put down her spade. She fetched her work bench, her toolbox and some wood. She measured and sawed and hammered and planed. She planed and hammered and sawed and measured.

Floyd came over to watch. "Do you want any help with what you're making?" he asked. "Because I've finished jumping."

Ruby didn't answer.

"What *are* you making, Ruby?" Floyd asked.

Still Ruby didn't answer.

"It's a boat," said Columbine. "We're all going to sea."

"It's not a boat, it's a fox trap," Crinkle said.

"Funny sort of fox trap," Floyd said. "It won't catch many foxes."

"It's not a fox trap, is it?" Cluck asked. "Is it something just for me?"

Ruby shook her head.

"For me, perhaps?" asked Floyd. "A kind of manger?"

Ruby shook her head again.

The Gargoyle knew what Ruby was making. But he said nothing.

Presently, Ruby fetched a tin of blue paint and began to write a sign. Ruby's Remarkable she wrote in blue letters.

Floyd watched.

Ruby went indoors and came back out with a little tin of red paint. Swap Shop she wrote in red.

"Oh. I see," said Floyd. But he didn't.

The Gargoyle saw, but he said nothing.

That night Ruby made apple pie for everyone. She took a bowlful, with extra cream, up by ladder to the Gargoyle. Ruby, Floyd and the hens ate theirs under the apple tree by the light of the yellow moon.

The next day was market day. Ruby's neighbours came down the lane carrying things to sell. A party from downstream passed by with bunches of watercress. The Rook Wood crowd carried mushrooms in their hats. The meadow people brought cowslips and honey. Hedgefolk had sacks full of old man's beard and rosehip syrup sealed in snailshells.

Ruby carried her invention out and set it up outside the garden gate.

It wasn't a boat.

Or a fox trap.

Or a manger.

It was a shop.

"What sort of shop?" asked Crinkle.

"A Swap Shop," Ruby told her.

"A what?" asked the hens.

The Gargoyle smiled. He knew what Ruby meant.

"Tell me something you like, but haven't got," said Ruby. "And then tell me something you've got, but don't want."

"Crumbs," said Cluck.

"Wet feathers," said Columbine, who had fallen in the Weedwater.

"I don't understand," said Crinkle.

Ruby shook her head. "You'll have to wait and see," she said.

Floyd helped her carry out the box of things she'd taken from the attic. They were, in case you have forgotten:

three velvet hats
a drum
a frying pan
a wasps' nest
three bats, all sleeping
two boots and one shoe
six packets of seeds

But no brocade ice skates.

Ruby arranged them on top of the counter. Floyd picked a bunch of daisies with his teeth and arranged them in an egg cup to make the shop look nice.

Ruby asked everybody what they wanted and wrote down what they said. This is what she wrote:-

Wanted:

books – no boring ones

telescope

top quality oil

things chickens like

She had to guess 'telescope' for the Gargoyle because he wouldn't say. And she put *things chickens like* because the hens could not agree.

Underneath she wrote:-

Help Yourselves

Please leave your swaps under the counter

Then she waited.

Floyd and the hens and the Gargoyle waited too.

All the neighbours stopped to look at *Ruby's Remarkable Swap Shop*. Every now and then somebody found something they wanted. Everyone who took something, left something. At the end of the day the only things left on top of the counter were:

the wasps' nest

and three bats – still sleeping

Underneath it were:

half a tin of engine oil

no telescope – but one pair of spectacles

an empty box with *worms – hens like these* written on the lid (the lid had come off and the worms had escaped)

a cabbage leaf, full of cake crumbs
and Three Beautiful Books:
Ghost Ship on the Weedwater
Journey to Rook Wood
Mysteries of the Meadow
So everyone was happy. Especially the
worms.

DEAREST RUBY RED

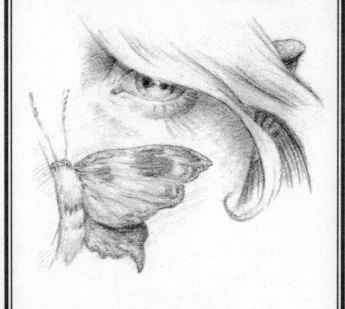

DEAREST RUBY RED

It was a soft autumn evening. Ruby lay in a nest of old man's beard and looked up through the twigs and branches of the apple tree to where an apple hung beside the moon. She liked to sleep outdoors on fine nights.

She read one chapter of her book – it was *Ghost Ship on the Weedwater*. Then she blew out her candle and went to sleep.

The Gargoyle looked down at her and smiled. *No sleep for me tonight,* he thought. *Not a wink, not a blink. I'll stay awake all night and watch over my Ruby.* And he did.

In the morning he struck six and fell fast asleep. Ruby woke up. She yawned and stretched and took a look around. There was a hat bobbing down the lane. Underneath the hat was Ruby's cousin Bellbine.

Bellbine lived in a tree house a mile or two downstream. Once in a while Ruby would float down and visit him. Once in a while, he'd walk up and visit her. This time he'd brought a small black goat with him.

Ruby kissed Bellbine hello and made him breakfast. The goat, whose name was

Rocket, pushed through the hedge into Floyd's meadow to find his own breakfast.

Bellbine had brought Ruby a letter from her grandfather. This is what it said:-

Dearest Ruby Red,

Would you undertake to make a journey for me? I would go myself but my legs are not what they were.

Please go to Grandma Samphire. Tell her I'm sorry that I wouldn't wash my socks. Tell her if she'll return this side of winter, I'll set all to rights. Tell her she must come soon, for the long sleep of winter calls when once the year is on the wane.

Tell her to come again.
Persuade her, Dearest Ruby Red.
Your Loving Grandpa,
Sweet William xxx

PS Tell her she'll find me in the windmill.
PPS Socks is the Signal, Ruby,
when All shall be Well.

"Will you come with me, Bellbine?" Ruby asked.

Bellbine shook his head. "Not me. I took a message to Grandma Samphire once before. She threw a saucepan at me."

Ruby went to the meadow gate and leant over. Floyd and Rocket were chasing one another round the meadow.

"Will you come with me?" Ruby called to Floyd.

"I can't," Floyd said. "I have to chase Rocket."

"Some friend *you're* turning out to be!" said Ruby.

She packed a hammock, a kite, a round ring, a white hankie, a red pen and plenty of biscuits. She said goodbye to the hens and the Gargoyle, but not to

Floyd or Rocket, and set off upstream.

The Gargoyle watched Ruby until her red hair disappeared behind a clump of rushes. Far and beyond he saw a silver glint. That was Grandma Samphire's lake. In the middle of the lake he saw a green dot. That was Grandma Samphire's island. Out of the green dot rose a blue wisp. That was the smoke from Grandma Samphire's cooking fire.

Away and beyond that, on top of a hill, the wind spun the sails of a windmill.

All day Ruby walked beside the Weedwater. In the evening she slung her hammock between the stream and a cornfield. All night she slept with the lap-lap of the stream in one ear and the rustle-bustle of the corn in the other.

In the morning she had biscuits for breakfast and away she went, following the Weedwater up to Grandma Samphire's lake. Round about midday she came to the pebbly edge of it. Grandma Samphire's island was out in the middle. It was round and green with a beach of white sand.

Ruby sat down by the side of the lake and wrote in red pen on her hankie:

AHOY THERE GRANDMA...
THIS IS RUBY

She tied the hankie to the ring, then threaded the ring onto the kite string. A breeze sprang up just as she needed one and carried the kite up high. The hankie ran up the kite string on its little round ring.

Presently, a rowing boat left the island and headed for the shore. It was rowed by someone small and wiry with hands like nutcrackers. That was Grandma Samphire. She hugged Ruby and Ruby hugged her back.

"Can I row us out to the island, Grandma?" Ruby asked.

"No," said Grandma Samphire. "Last time I let you row, you tipped us out."

"That was ages ago," said Ruby.

"But I have not forgotten it," said Grandma Samphire. "I've only just dried out."

Ruby did not mention Sweet William's message at once. She waited until after supper. Grandma Samphire cooked sorrel soup and roast crab apples.

They ate on the beach beside a driftwood fire. After supper, Grandma Samphire played her squeeze box. When she was sleepy, Ruby hung her hammock beside Grandma Samphire's and they both settled down for the night.

"I suppose you've got a message for me, Ruby Red," said Grandma Samphire, pulling on her red flannel bed jacket.

"Yes, Grandma," said Ruby.

"I suppose it's from Sweet William."

"Yes, Grandma," said Ruby.

"You may as well tell me what it is. Though I don't promise to listen."

Ruby looked across to make certain that her grandmother had nothing handy to throw. "He sent you a letter, Grandma," she said.

"Letter's no good to me. I've lost my glasses."

"He's sorry that he wouldn't wash his socks, Grandma."

"Hmmmph!" said Grandma Samphire.

She didn't say anything else, so Ruby curled into her hammock and slept.

Next morning, after a breakfast of lake-lily pancakes, Grandma Samphire rowed Ruby back to the mainland and they kissed goodbye.

"What about Grandpa?" Ruby asked.

"What *about* him?" Grandma Samphire answered, rooting about in the bottom of her boat for something to throw. Ruby ran off, blowing her grandmother a kiss.

She decided to visit her grandfather

anyway, message or no message. His windmill was close by, on top of a hill overlooking the lake. It was a steep way up to the top and what with stopping for rests, it was nearly tea-time when Ruby knocked on the windmill door.

There was no answer.

Ruby knocked again. Still no answer.

Ruby could hear her grandfather snoring. She picked up a handful of pebbles and tossed them up at his bedroom window.

Ruby heard a grunt and a snuffle. Sweet William opened his window and leant out. He was small and old and his beard came down almost to the ground, although his bedroom was three floors up.

"Ruby Red," he smiled. "My

favourite granddaughter. Is that you? Make yourself comfortable, and put the kettle on. It's weeks since anybody made a cup of tea round here."

Ruby made tea and toast. Then she sat down and gave her grandfather a long, hard look.

"Bellbine came to see me," she said. "He brought your letter for Grandma Samphire."

"Did you take it to her, Ruby?"

"Yes, Grandpa."

"Did she like it?"

"She didn't throw anything. But she sent no reply."

Sweet William sniffed. A tear trickled down into his beard.

"Why don't you wash your socks, Grandpa?" Ruby asked. "If that's all

Grandma Samphire wants?"

"I don't know how," Sweet William answered.

"Just put them in the bath," Ruby advised. "I'll show you what to do."

Sweet William filled his bath with hot water and tipped in his socks. There were twenty-seven pairs, and five odd ones.

"Now what?" he asked.

"Get in with them and walk about," Ruby suggested.

Sweet William rolled up his trouser legs and got in. The bath water turned brown and muddy. Ruby made him change it several times.

"Will you look at my feet?" he exclaimed, when the water was clear enough for him to see them. "They've gone all wrinkly, Ruby. I think they've shrunk!"

"Never mind, Grandpa," said Ruby. "I expect your socks have too."

She rigged up a clothes line on the sails of the windmill. Sweet William pulled the levers that worked the sails to bring them down low, while Ruby pegged out his socks.

After that it was bedtime.

In the morning Ruby said goodbye to her grandfather and set off for home. When she got to the bottom of the hill she looked back. There were fifty-nine socks going round with the sails of the windmill.

Well, it's a start, she thought.

When she got home, Ruby found Floyd and Rocket in the middle of a quarrel. Rocket had eaten Floyd's best patch of meadowsweet without asking.

"How can you be so *greedy*?" stamped Floyd.

"How can you be so *selfish*?" snapped Rocket.

He butted Floyd in the side and Floyd bit him.

The Gargoyle closed both eyes and raised his eyebrows.

Ruby shook her head. "Why is everybody fighting?" she asked.

"Never mind them," called Bellbine from the kitchen. "Come and have some Welcome Home Cake."

"Can it be Goodbye Cake as well as Welcome Home Cake?" Floyd asked, glowering at Rocket.

"It can be Anything You Like Cake," said Bellbine.

"Will there be crumbs?" asked Cluck.

Ruby laid the table, Bellbine put the cake in the middle and everybody came to tea.

Ruby fetched a ladder and climbed up with a slice for the Gargoyle. From the top of the ladder she could see a glint of silver. That was Grandma Samphire's lake. In the middle of the silver she could see a green dot. That was Grandma Samphire's island.

Away and beyond, on top of a hill, the sails of Sweet William's windmill went round and round.

Fifty-nine socks flew from the sails.

And one red flannel bed jacket.

FIRECRACKER FLY

FIRECRACKER FLY

Deep down dark in the middle of the night, Ruby woke up. She hopped out of her hammock and went to her small round window. The moon hung full and fat above Floyd's meadow. Over on the far side of the meadow, Ruby saw a flickering bonfire.

Ruby climbed out of the window and let herself down to the ground on the ivy. She crept quietly past the hen coop without waking Columbine, Crinkle or Cluck. She slipped over the meadow gate and ran out into the long wet grass.

When she got close to the fire, she saw that there was someone sitting beside it. Someone smallish. He had long black hair tied back in a plait, and he was toasting something on the end of a sword. A small green parrot perched on his shoulder.

"Firecracker Fly at your service, Signorina," he said, rising and bowing.

"Ruby Red at yours," said Ruby politely. "You look like Fandango Fly – I've got a book of his adventures."

The stranger smiled. "Old Fandango was my grandpa. This here is his parrot – name of Fernanda Fly." The parrot bobbed her head politely. "Old Fandango and me, we sailed the Weedwater together many a moony night. He's gone now, is old Fandango. Gone to look for gold somewhere beyond the moon. Firecracker sails alone these days – excepting for Fernanda."

"I thought you'd be bigger," Ruby said. "Fandango was bigger, in his picture."

"We're a dwindling family, that's what. Dwindling and dark. Flys are night people. Pirating's night work. Wants the dark."

"Have you no family, now your grandpa's gone?" asked Ruby.

"Only my sisters, Fancy and Foxy Fly. But I steer clear of them. They're after me to settle down but that won't do for me. A pirate's life is what I like, Signorina."

"Who do you steal from?" Ruby asked.

"*Steal from? Steal from??* Firecracker Fly don't steal!"

"I'm sorry, Firecracker. I thought that's what pirates did."

"Firecracker Fly's as honest as the night is dark."

Ruby looked round. The moon lit up all but the furthest corners of the meadow. The night wasn't dark at all.

"I do a little trading. Fish a little. Time was, Flys was known through the five oceans of the world. But now we're river folk. Stream folk, you might say. The Weedwater's my home. Would you

care for a cruise aboard the good ship
Fly-by-Night?"

"I certainly would," said Ruby.

"First we'll souse the fire. Don't want
to set the field alight."

Firecracker dipped up ditch water in
his hat and tipped it over the bonfire.
The flames sputtered and went out.
Fernanda sneezed and took off from his
shoulder.

"You go on aboard, old lady,"
Firecracker told the parrot. "Can't have
you catching cold."

"Can she find the way in the dark?"
Ruby asked.

"*Find the way*? *Find the way*?!
Fernanda Fly's her name, travelling's her
game. That bird come out of the egg
with a compass in her head!"

Fernanda flapped off over the meadow, leaving Ruby and Firecracker to follow on foot. Presently Ruby could hear the voice of the Weedwater, which sang louder by night than by day, as all streams do.

The *Fly-by-Night* was moored to a tree root. A narrow gangplank led from bank to deck. Ruby followed Firecracker on board.

The *Fly-by-Night* was more like a houseboat than a pirate ship. She had a small patched sail for lake work. On the stream, Firecracker punted her with a long pole. There was no galley — Firecracker came ashore to cook his supper on an open fire — but there was a cabin for his hammock and an armchair in which he sat to write up his memoirs of an evening.

Firecracker took out a chart of the Weedwater and studied it. "We'll float down to the Rook Wood Pool," he said. "It's a good place for a midnight swim — and it's a fine ferny place to hide up during the day."

"Who do you hide from, in the day time?" asked Ruby.

"My two sisters," Firecracker replied. "Fancy and Foxy Fly. They live down river in a suitcase. They'd like to see me shore-bound if they could only catch me. But I can't abide to be shut in."

Firecracker cast off from the tree root, and away went the *Fly-by-Night*, dipping and bobbing down the stream. Moon-dapple hid her when the breeze ruffled the leaves overhead. When the wind dropped and the leaves grew still, she

reappeared, riding the current proudly.

It was a pleasant trip downstream. But just as Rook Wood Pool came into view, there was a grating, grinding noise. Fernanda squawked a warning – too late – and the *Fly-by-Night* shuddered, shook, and stuck fast on a sandy spit of gravel.

"Blam and darst it, this is what I hate!" exclaimed Firecracker. "Stuck fast! Run aground!" He rolled up his trousers and hopped overboard. He pushed and shoved and grunted and gasped but he couldn't shift the boat.

Ruby tucked up her nightdress and jumped down to help.

Firecracker threw a line to Fernanda, who tried towing. But they could not shift the *Fly-by-Night*.

"Mercy on me!" Firecracker moaned. "It'll be light in two flicks of a fishtail! All it will take is for Fancy and Foxy to trundle by and I'll be done for! What *am* I going to do, Ruby Red?"

"Give me a pencil and paper, quick!" said Ruby.

Firecracker did.

Dear Floyd,

I am on board the good ship Fly-by-Night.

We are stuck in the shallows just by the Rook Wood Pool.

Please come at once and tow us off.

Best love,

Ruby.

PS Come at once!

PPS Hurry!

Ruby rolled the letter up and gave it to Fernanda, who flapped away through the dawn light, carrying the message safely in her beak.

The sun was rising and the stream was starting to wake up before Ruby and Firecracker heard the thudding of small hooves galloping towards them.

At the same moment, two fussy voices could be heard approaching from Rook Wood.

"If *only* we could find that feckless Firecracker," Fancy was saying, "we could make him mend the lock on our suitcase."

"And polish up the handle," Foxy added.

"And wash the windows," Fancy said.

"And sweep the chimney."

"And cut the grass."

"And do all the things that we don't want to do. Where *is* that lazy lout?"

"Save me!" sobbed Firecracker, hiding behind Ruby. "Help!"

Floyd skidded to a halt on the river bank. Ruby leapt ashore with a rope and tied it round Floyd's neck. Floyd began to heave. His shiny tin muscles rippled and shone in the morning light, and his silver tail trembled. His neck arched as he took the weight of the good ship *Fly-by-Night* on his chest. Slow and steady, strong and sure, he tugged her off the gravel and towed her in towards the bank. Silently she glided into deep water and vanished underneath the overhanging ferns – just as Firecracker's sisters swept round the corner, still complaining.

Quick as a flash, Ruby hopped onto Floyd's back. "Home, Floyd!" she whispered.

Floyd snorted. His sharp tin hooves pawed at the river bank. He lifted his head and neighed his loudest, proudest neigh.

Foxy and Fancy Fly took one look at him – and ran.

Floyd dashed away at a gallop. Down the river bank, over hedges and ditches, across the morning meadow, and safe home into Ruby's garden – where the Gargoyle was just striking his favourite six.

THE
SNOW PICNIC

THE SNOW PICNIC

It was a cold, dark night, as sharp as splinters. The Gargoyle loved the cold snow and the clear sky and the winding lane in winter.

Floyd had moved indoors with Ruby. The hens had come in too. So had a wren, as well as a hedgehog who couldn't sleep. They made quite a crowd round Ruby's fireside.

Ruby was making something.

"What is it Ruby?" Floyd asked. "Is it a present for me?"

"Skates," Ruby said. "Two pairs for you and a pair each for the hens."

Hen's skates need four long toe parts, three at the front and one at the back. They must fit snugly round the ankles, or the hens will wobble. Ruby lined everybody's boots with moss, so they wouldn't rub. Her own skates were the red brocade ones she had found in the attic.

She oiled all twelve skates and put them in the log basket. Then she ran out to hear the Gargoyle strike ten. He struck it with difficulty because of the icicles hanging from his hinge. But he was not one to give up.

"We're going on a picnic tomorrow,

Gargoyle," Ruby told him. "Floyd and the hens are coming too. Don't tell the hens or they'll *never* get to sleep."

The Gargoyle sighed. As if he would tell the hens anything. Ruby blew a kiss up to him on a cloud of white breath.

Indoors, Floyd stood beside the fire and wondered about things. *How does ice get so hard?* he wondered. *What if air did that? We'd all be stuck.* He shook his ears. *Life's full of mysteries,* he thought.

Ruby's little house grew warm and quiet. Columbine, Crinkle and Cluck had settled on the mantelpiece. The hedgehog had curled up in the kindling. Deep inside Ruby's sewing box, the wren crept into a ball of wool.

Ruby climbed the ladder to her bedroom. There were frost flowers on her window and her hammock was dusted with snow. She took her quilt and went back down the ladder. She put the last log on the fire and curled up on the hearth rug next to Floyd.

When the Gargoyle struck six next morning, nobody woke. They were all too warm and comfortable. The Gargoyle would have liked to strike six again but he couldn't, so he snoozed until seven and then he struck it extra hard.

Ruby hopped outside with her quilt round her shoulders.

"We all slept in," she said. "Especially the hedgehog. He's crawled into a sock he found under the table. Isn't it good picnic weather, Gargoyle?"

The Gargoyle stared up at the yellow snow clouds. He didn't say a thing. But

Ruby knew what he was thinking.

"Don't worry, Gargoyle. We'll be back before the snow falls," she promised.

Some time later, five little figures came out through the front door directly below the Gargoyle and made their way down to the frozen Weedwater. The Gargoyle watched them for a while, then shook his head, dislodging an icicle that had formed under his nose.

Ruby helped the hens on with their skates and did up their laces. They stepped daintily onto the ice and stood quite still, clucking softly.

Floyd stamped his skates on by himself. He took a run at the ice and jumped on. "Look at me!" he shouted happily.

The Gargoyle watched him shoot across the stream and crash into the bank.

"Away we go," said Ruby. "One, two, and glide."

Ruby could skate backwards, forwards and sideways. She could do the quickstep, the fox-trot and the waltz.

"The waltz looks nice," said Columbine to Crinkle. "Shall we dance?"

Columbine and Crinkle danced gently into Cluck. Cluck glided into Floyd and Floyd sat down suddenly on the ice.

The Gargoyle chuckled quietly but Ruby stamped with her red brocade skates on the ice.

"Skating is supposed to be graceful!" she said. "Get up all of you!"

Soon everyone was quite warm from falling down and getting up, but Ruby wouldn't let them take their hats or scarves off.

"That's how you catch a chill," she warned. Floyd snorted, but he kept his scarf on.

"Where are we going?" Columbine asked.

"To Rook Wood. For a snow picnic."

Columbine looked doubtfully at the pale winter sun. A luminous white ring shone round it.

> *Ring round the sun,*
> *A storm will come,*
> *Ring round the moon,*
> *Travellers' doom,*

she clucked.

"There won't be a storm in Rook Wood, Columbine," said Ruby. "There never is. And we're certainly not doomed. Come on."

The frozen pathway of the Weedwater gleamed icily. High in the sky an east wind shook the treetops. It blew the rooks about the sky like specks of soot. Underneath the branches of Rook Wood the snow lay flat and calm.

"Skates off," said Ruby, when they got there. "Cluck, look for chestnuts. Columbine and Crinkle, you find fir cones."

"We don't eat fir cones," Columbine said. "We eat worms."

"And crumbs," said Cluck.

"The fir cones are for a fire," Ruby

told them. "You always have a fire at a snow picnic."

The hens collected fir cones and Floyd built a fire. Ruby lit it and popped Cluck's chestnuts in to roast. She spread the picnic rug out on the snow and arranged cake and biscuits round a flask of cherry brandy. She stuck a candle in a snowball and lit it. Everything was ready.

"Ruby," said Floyd, "I'm starving. Can we start?"

The picnic was a success. Everybody liked what they had to eat and nobody forgot to pass things. Afterwards they sat and watched the snowflakes floating past the candle flame. Presently an extra large flake landed right on top of it, making it spit and fizzle.

Ruby got up and went to the edge of

the wood to peep out. Everything outside the wood looked different. The frozen Weedwater had vanished. The banks had vanished. The fields had vanished. Ruby walked slowly back to the fire. "There's nothing but snow outside the wood," she said.

"Just as I feared," said Columbine. "We're doomed." A tear trickled down to the end of her beak and hung there like a hailstone.

"We're all going to die!" sobbed Cluck.

"What shall we do?" cried Crinkle.

"We'll build an igloo," Ruby said.

It's not hard to make an igloo if you know how, and Ruby did. Floyd scooped up piles of snow, the hens pecked them into blocks and Ruby stacked them up into a smooth white dome. When she had put the last block in place, everyone went inside.

Five faces peeped out through the small round door and watched the wood fill up with snow. One by one they settled themselves down on the picnic rug and nodded off.

Presently, all that could be heard coming from the igloo were three light snores, one middling snore and a rumble.

Deep in the dark of night, Ruby woke up. She stuck her head out through the doorway and stared. The wood was lit by moonlight. The sky looked large and cold and bright. High and beyond, stars twinkled. Ruby crept back to Floyd's warm side and slept.

In the morning there was no way of telling which way was home. The snow lay thick and deep in all directions.

"We're lost," said Crinkle. "Lost, in a sea of snow."

"No one will ever find us," sniffed Cluck.

"We'll never see our coop again," said Columbine.

"Shush!" said Ruby. "Listen!"

Far away across the countryside the Gargoyle was striking six.

"Lucky Gargoyle," said Columbine.

"Lucky, lucky him," said Cluck.

"*He* isn't lost," said Crinkle.

"Neither are we," said Ruby. "Come on."

She climbed onto Floyd's back and they set off slowly, heading towards the sound of the Gargoyle's last strike.

The hens were light enough to walk over the top of the snow without sinking in, but for Floyd it was a long, hard journey. He ploughed through the snow with his four tin legs and he never once complained, not even when the snow came half-way up his chest. He just shook it out of his ears, blinked it out of his eyes, and plodded on.

Every now and then, they took a wrong turning, or fell into a snow drift. Columbine, Crinkle and Cluck made a fuss each time but Floyd never faltered.

"That Floyd's a wonder," Cluck said.

"He certainly is," said Crinkle.

"Who would have thought it?" Columbine asked, rather rudely.

"I would," said Ruby. "I always knew

Floyd was no ordinary horse. Floyd, you're a Hero."

Floyd blushed, and struggled on.

And every hour, on the hour, the Gargoyle struck.

Each time he struck, he sounded louder.

By the time he got to ten o'clock, the travellers could see the roof of Ruby's house.

Soon after that, they saw the Gargoyle himself, covered in snow and icicles, bonging away with his mallet.

"Thank you Gargoyle," Ruby said, when at last she stood beneath him. "You struck us all the way home."

"I always will," said the Gargoyle.

The End